For Michael Philip
J.C.

For Amelia
S.L.

Text copyright © 1995 by June Crebbin
Illustrations copyright © 1995 by Stephen Lambert

First U.S. edition 1995

Library of Congress Cataloging-in-Publication Data

Crebbin, June.
The train ride / June Crebbin ; illustrated by
Stephen Lambert. — 1st U.S. ed.
Summary: A journey on a train provides excitement,
nice scenery, and pleasant anticipation.
ISBN 1-56402-546-2
[1. Railroads— Fiction.] I. Lambert, Stephen,
1964 –   ill. II. Title.
PZ7.C86Tr   1995
[E]—dc20   94-15156

10 9 8 7 6 5 4 3 2 1

Printed in Belgium

The pictures in this book were done in chalk pastel.

Candlewick Press
2067 Massachusetts Avenue
Cambridge, Massachusetts 02140

The Train Ride

by
June Crebbin

CANDLEWICK PRESS
CAMBRIDGE, MASSACHUSETTS

illustrated by
Stephen Lambert

We're off on a journey   Out of the town —

What shall I see? What shall I see?

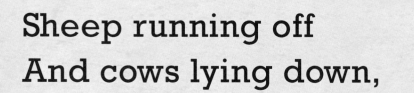

Sheep running off
And cows lying down,

That's what I see,
That's what I see.

Over the meadow,
Up on the hill,

What shall I see?
What shall I see?

A mare and her foal
Standing perfectly still,

That's what I see,
That's what I see.

There is a farm
Down a bumpety road —

What shall I see?
What shall I see?

A shiny red tractor
Pulling its load,

That's what I see,
That's what I see.

Here in my seat,
My lunch on my knee,

What shall I see?
What shall I see?

A ticket collector
Smiling at me,

That's what I see,
That's what I see.

Into the tunnel,
Scary and black,

What shall I see?
What shall I see?

My face in a mirror,
Staring back,

That's what I see,
That's what I see.

After the tunnel,
When we come out,

What shall I see?
What shall I see?

A gaggle of geese
Strutting about,

That's what I see,
That's what I see.

Over the treetops,
High in the sky,

What shall I see?
What shall I see?

A giant balloon
Sailing by,

That's what I see,
That's what I see.

Listen! The engine
Is slowing down —

What shall I see?
What shall I see?

A market square,
A seaside town,

That's what I see,
That's what I see.

There is the lighthouse,   The sand, and the sea . . .

Here is the station —

Whom shall I see?

There is my grandma

Welcoming me . . .

Welcoming

me.